Words to Know Before

basketball

catch

chase

dance

dive

ducks

shape

stretch

swim

walk

www.rourkeeducationalmedia.com

Edited by Luana Mitten
Illustrated by John Reasoner
Art Direction and Page Layout by Renee Brady

Scan for Related Titles
and Teacher Resources

Library of Congress PCN Data

Buff Ducks / Precious McKenzie
ISBN 978-1-61810-171-6 (hard cover) (alk. paper)
ISBN 978-1-61810-304-8 (soft cover)
ISBN 978-1-61810-426-7 (eBook)
Library of Congress Control Number: 2012936763

Rourke Educational Media
Printed in the United States of America,
North Mankato, Minnesota

Also Available as:

Educational Media

rourkeeducationalmedia.com

customerservice@rourkeeducationalmedia.com • PO Box 643328 Vero Beach, Florida 32964

Buff Ducks

By Precious McKenzie

Illustrated by John Reasoner

Ducks get in shape.

4

Ducks stretch. Ducks bend.

Ducks walk.

Ducks waddle.
Ducks run.

8

Ducks dive. Ducks float.
Ducks swim.

Ducks splash.

11

Ducks shimmy. Ducks shake. Ducks dance.

13

Ducks dash.

Ducks chase.
Ducks tag.

Ducks catch.
Ducks throw.

Ducks play basketball.

Buff ducks!

After Reading Activities

You and the Story...

What did the ducks do before they exercised?
How many different activities did the ducks do to stay in shape?
Do you like to exercise?
What activities do you like to do to stay healthy?

Words You Know Now...

Can you find a word with a short u sound like in the word pup?
Can you find a word with a long a sound like in the word cape?

basketball	ducks
catch	shape
chase	stretch
dance	swim
dive	walk

You Could...Act Out Buff Ducks at Your House or School

- Ask a friend to act out the story with you.

- Work together to make duck masks and wings.

- Decide which duck each person will be during the show.

- Gather together to make props.

- Practice your play.

- Invite your friends and family to see your play.

About the Author

Precious McKenzie loves to write funny stories about animals. Precious lives with her husband and three children in Montana. She likes to go for walks and watch the ducks play.

Meet The Author!
www.meetREMauthors.com

About the Illustrator

John Reasoner has loved to draw ever since he was a little kid. He lives in Colorado Springs with his fiance and two dogs, Bumble and Wiggum. He gets his inspiration from walking his dogs through the local parks and playing with his niece and nephew. When not illustrating, John can be found playing his favorite video games!